BBT's BARBERSHOP: SEASON ONE

Ten cuts. Ten convos. One chair.

by

BRIAN TURNER

For permissions, inquiries, or bulk orders, please contact:
✉ hi@heybbt.com
🌐 www.heybbt.com

First Edition
ISBN: 979-8-9995161-3-8

Cover design by Leonardo.ai, with final layout by Brian Turner
Interior layout by Brian Turner and team

Printed in the United States of America

Table of Contents

dedication.

To Bryce,

You are my greatest joy, my fiercest inspiration, and
the reason I keep going.
Your questions make me better, your dreams keep
me honest,
and your heart reminds me of what matters most.
May you always know your worth, chase your
passions boldly,
and remember that your story is powerful beyond
measure.

To my Bria, aka 'Bri Bri,'

Your light, kindness, and determination brighten
even my darkest days.
Your laughter is proof that hope is real,
and your courage shows me what resilience truly
looks like.
May you never doubt how loved you are or how
strong your voice can be.

And to every father, son, and daughter searching for understanding
May these conversations remind you that it's never too late to talk,
never too soon to listen,
and always the perfect time to grow together.

And to my grandma,
In the quietest moments,
your prayers built bridges I couldn't see.
Your laughter softened storms I couldn't escape.
Your love made impossible dreams feel real.
And though your hands can't hold me now,
your faith still lifts me higher than I ever thought I could reach.

Marie Simmons —

I always knew I would honor you in a public way, but I never knew how.
Thank you for believing in me, for pushing me, and for helping me see I could do more than I ever dreamed.
You made me the crazy, risk-taking entrepreneur I am today.
I know I can never truly fail with you as my guardian angel watching over me.

Bria Marie is named after you, and I see your light shining through her every day.
Keep guiding us. Keep protecting us.

And thank you for showing me what unstoppable love looks like.

introduction.

A father.
A son.
A barbershop where every cut comes with a story.

Some of these stories happened.
Some almost happened.
Some probably shouldn't have happened.

But each one has something to say
about surviving,
laughing,
and learning to keep your head up when life tries to
knock you down.

The barbershop is where truth shows up uninvited,
jokes keep it from getting too heavy,
and a kid starts piecing together how the world
really works.

This isn't a sermon.
It's a seat in the chair.

So get comfortable.
The clippers are humming.
Next cut's about to begin.

Welcome to *BBT's Barbershop*.
Let's talk.

failure.

The sun crawled over rooftops as the neighborhood woke up. A few stray dogs barked. A bus groaned to a stop down the block. And the air carried the promise of a day that could break you, or make you.

Brian unlocked the door to BBT's Barbershop, head high but eyes tired. He flipped on the lights, and the mirrors caught a man trying to hold everything together. He straightened the chairs, swept away yesterday's hair, and took a deep breath.

If it wasn't your money, it was your health. If it wasn't your health, it was something else. Life didn't stop testing you, but that didn't mean you ever stopped fighting.

He woke up every day knowing the world was waiting to punch him in the face. But he still opened those doors.

Bryce hopped into the chair with his usual swagger, but the smirk on his face faded when he caught his father's reflection in the mirror. His dad looked like he'd lost something he couldn't afford to lose.

"Dad, what's wrong?" Bryce asked quietly. "You look like you just lost your last chicken wing."

Brian cracked a tired smile. "Better my wing than my peace of mind."

The front door swung open with a squeak. Leon and Jackie strolled in, bringing the morning's chaos with them.

"What happened, B?" Leon called out, eyes glinting with mischief. "Somebody steal your hairline?"

Brian raised his clippers, eyes narrowed but amused. "Keep talking, Leon. You're next in this chair."

Jackie snorted. "Man's got that look—like he spent the night Googling how to sell a kidney.."

Leon slapped Jackie's shoulder. "Don't give him ideas. Brian's liable to put that on Facebook Marketplace."

The shop echoed with laughter. Bryce giggled along, but his eyes kept flicking to his dad. He could see the strain hidden behind the jokes.

Jackie caught Bryce's worried glance. "Don't let him fool you, kid. Your dad's always looked rough in the morning."

Brian started on Bryce's haircut. The clippers buzzed a steady rhythm, but the words that came were anything but light.

"Mortgage's falling behind," Brian said softly, almost to himself. "Eviction letters show up faster than paychecks."

"Really?" Bryce asked, voice small. "I didn't know it was that bad."

Brian paused, hand resting gently on his son's head. "But a roof doesn't make a home. We're family, no matter where we sleep."

He kept cutting, his voice calm, every word deliberate. "Marriage? Love's simple when life is. But when everything's on fire, that's when you find out if it's real.."

Bryce swallowed hard. "You and Mom... do you fight because of me?"

"No, son," Brian said firmly. "Not because of you. Life's just heavy sometimes."

Brian's eyes shifted to the mirror, his own reflection glaring back at him. "Business? Contracts are ending. Employees gotta eat, gotta get paid. It's not easy knowing other people's families depend on me showing up every day."

Bryce looked stunned. "So you still have to pay everyone, even when there's no money?"

"Every last one," Brian said. "That's what responsibility looks like."

Brian smirked and lifted Bryce's chin. "Being broke teaches you things. Like how ketchup can be pasta sauce, soup, or pizza topping."

Bryce scrunched his nose. "Ketchup ramen? Gross, Dad."

Leon burst out laughing. "That's gourmet, bro. Call it Chef Boyar-Broke."

From the corner, Jackie chimed in, his voice warm. "Tell him, Brian. Ramen nights build character."

The laughter died down. Bryce's eyes grew serious. "You always seem happy," he whispered. "How do you hide it?"

Brian exhaled slowly. "Because I have to. **You don't get to see me break.** That's my job as your dad."

He ruffled Bryce's hair, smiling faintly. "I don't tell you this to scare you. I tell you so you know what standing tall looks like when life tries to knock you down."

"You're the strongest man I know," Bryce said, eyes wide.

Brian's smile grew a little stronger. "That's because I taught you everything you know."

Brian's eyes drifted past the mirrors, lost in memory. "You want to know why I don't break? Why I don't let fear show?"

In his mind, he saw Grandma's kitchen. Young Brian hugging her waist, her eyes sharp and full of fire.

"I don't care if you're tired, boy," her voice echoed. "You're gonna be the best."

"She made me who I am," Brian murmured. "Even now, I hear her voice when I feel like giving up."

Bryce leaned forward, eyes burning with curiosity. "So... how'd you get like this?"

Brian lowered his clippers, locking eyes with his son. "That story starts in a place called DC, back when the world looked a whole lot different."

Bryce couldn't wait to hear more, but he had no idea how deep the story of *misfortune* would go.

misfortune.

The barbershop was alive with morning energy. Clippers buzzed, the faint smell of alcohol spray hung in the air, and sunlight crawled across the black-and-white checkered floor. Leon kicked back in his chair, Jackie scrolled through her phone, and Trey leaned in the doorway, each adding their own flavor to the morning banter.

Bryce shifted nervously under the cape, watching his father's face in the mirror. The laughter and jokes around him couldn't hide the weight he'd felt since yesterday. He cleared his throat.

His voice felt small in the middle of all the noise.

"Dad," Bryce asked, voice quiet but insistent, "was it always this bad?"

Brian raised an eyebrow, keeping his eyes on Bryce's reflection. "What do you mean?"

"Life. Like... were things always this hard for you?"

Leon walked in, flopping into his usual chair with a dramatic sigh. "Story time? Don't mind if I do."

Jackie appeared with her coffee, smirking as she settled into her spot. "Better be a good one, Brian."

Brian cracked a grin as he clicked the clippers on, the buzz filling the space with a steady hum. His voice dropped low. "Let me take y'all back... to 80s DC, when a kid like me had to learn fast, or not at all."

Leon leaned forward, eyes dancing. "You mean the Chocolate City days? Where the only sweet part was the name?"

Jackie shook her head, a wry smile on her lips. "Baby, back then, you prayed your block wasn't the next headline."

Trey chuckled from the doorway. "Man, I bet DC was wild, but not like today with cameras everywhere."

Brian shook his head slowly, eyes darkening with memory. "Nah... back then, you just hoped nobody saw you cry."

Bryce's eyes widened, leaning forward in the chair. "So what happened, Dad?"

Brian sighed, setting his clippers down with a soft clack. He rubbed his hands together, eyes drifting to the ceiling like he could see the past replaying there.

"You know, son," Brian began, voice steady but low, "where I grew up, you had to learn how to survive before you learned how to multiply. You had to watch every corner, every bus stop. DC wasn't a city; it was a battlefield."

He paused, eyes hardening as he stared into the mirror. "We were broke. And I don't mean the kind of broke where you can't get the new Jordans. I'm talking about ketchup sandwiches for dinner broke. I'm talking about opening the fridge and seeing just ice and a light bulb broke."

Jackie whistled low, shaking her head. "You know it's bad when the ketchup bottle looks like a gourmet meal."

Leon added, "Or when that one pack of ramen gotta last three days."

Brian cracked a tired smile, but his eyes never softened.

"We didn't just live in the hood; the hood lived in us.

You couldn't let people see you scared, because fear was a scent that traveled faster than blood in water."

He looked down at Bryce's wide eyes, seeing himself reflected in his son's innocence.

"Every day, walking to school felt like tiptoeing through a minefield. You had to know who was fighting with who, which corners to cross, which alleys to avoid. A wrong turn could mean you came home with a busted lip... or you didn't come home at all."

Brian's eyes grew distant, memories flooding in. "I remember going outside and all I heard were cop cars and ambulances, like the city's own twisted lullaby. Go-go music blared from boomboxes, giving DC its own heartbeat that echoed through every cracked sidewalk. Kids argued whether the Redskins would ever win another Super Bowl, or if the Georgetown Hoyas would finally bring home a championship. We'd talk big dreams, but everyone felt the chill when Len Bias's name hit the news—like hope itself overdosed overnight."

He shook his head slowly. "We didn't know the word *Reaganomics*, but we felt it every time Grandma counted out quarters at the grocery store, praying they'd stretch to the end of the week."

Bryce shifted uncomfortably, but Brian's voice carried on, unwavering. "And if you made it to school, you still had to figure out how to eat. The free lunch line? That line was a bullseye. Kids would clown you like it was their job. 'Look at him, can't even pay for his own food.' They'd laugh, but there was nothing funny about it when your stomach felt like it was eating itself."

Brian's eyes narrowed as old memories took over. "So I got smart. I learned how to flip coins at recess. A quarter here, a quarter there, heads or tails decided if I'd eat or go another day with an empty belly. It wasn't much, but I learned how to hustle before I learned long division."

Leon laughed, slapping the armrest of his chair. "Brian the Coin Hustler. I can see it now."

Jackie added with a grin, "Bet you had custom coins with your face on them."

Bryce giggled, but his voice was shaky. "So you... you gambled just to eat?"

Brian looked at him, eyes sharp but sad. "I did whatever I had to. Survival doesn't wait for you to figure things out. It just keeps moving."

The shop grew quiet, the only sounds the soft hum of the fluorescent lights and the distant rumble of a bus outside. Brian took a deep breath, eyes far away.

"One day, your great-grandma took me shopping," he said softly. "She knew my pants were falling apart, holes growing bigger every day. I hated going to school like that. She knew it too."

He swallowed hard. "She didn't have it, but she wanted me to feel like I belonged. So we went to this department store, and she picked up a pair of *Used Jeans*. Seventy bucks for a brand that literally said 'Used' on the tag. She slid her credit card across the counter, her hand shaking, knowing she'd be paying it off forever. But she did it anyway."

Bryce's eyes welled up. "Why would she do that?"

Brian's voice dropped to a whisper. "Because love, son. Love will make you spend money you don't have, fight battles you can't win, just so the people you care about can stand tall. She didn't want me to feel less than anyone else. She wanted me to know I was worth it."

Silence hung thick in the barbershop. Even Leon and Jackie lowered their eyes, memories of their own struggles flickering across their faces.

Bryce reached up, his small hand brushing his father's arm. "Is that why you never let me quit?"

Brian looked at him, a tear caught in the corner of his eye. "That's exactly why. You don't get to give up. Not when someone fought that hard for you to have a chance."

Bryce couldn't wait to hear more—but he had no idea how powerful Grandma's lesson would be.

grandma.

Morning light filtered through the barbershop windows, casting a golden glow over worn chairs and faded clippers. Leon flipped through a tattered magazine, Jackie sipped her coffee, and Trey leaned against the doorframe, eyes curious. The shop felt different today, quieter, softer, like it was waiting for the next story.

Bryce broke the silence. "Dad... if it was that rough, who kept you safe?"

Brian paused, his hands stilling on the clippers. His eyes grew distant, memories pulling him back decades. He took a slow breath.

"Grandma," he said, voice low but full of strength. "She was my rock. My forever protector."

Leon leaned forward, eyebrows raised. "You mean the grandma who could throw a shoe around a corner and still hit you?"

Jackie burst out laughing, nearly spilling her coffee. "Boy, grandmas *have* better aim than the Marines."

Brian cracked a grin, shaking his head. "Yeah, that was her. But it wasn't just the shoe. It was her faith. You'd be ready to quit, and she'd look you dead in the eye and say, 'Just pray, baby. The Lord didn't bring you this far to leave you.' Then two minutes later, she'd call somebody an old fool and tell them to get out her kitchen."

Bryce giggled, eyes wide. "She cussed?"

Brian chuckled. "She'd let one slip, sure. But even her curses felt like love."

He set the clippers down and leaned on the counter, voice growing softer. "When I was six, we moved from DC to PG County. Thought it'd be different, new streets, new houses, but PG was the same story in a different zip code. Drugs, fights, broken dreams, all waiting outside our door."

He looked up, eyes bright with memory. "But inside? Inside Grandma's house, it was a different world. The smell of fried chicken, sweet cornbread, and greens filled the air. Gospel music drifted through the halls. People were always around—friends, cousins, neighbors. Grandma never let anyone go hungry or sleep outside if she could help it. Her door was always open."

Brian's eyes softened. "She could do it all. She worked two, sometimes three jobs. She'd stretch a dollar until it begged for mercy. And when I'd come home crying because kids said I was poor, she'd kneel down, put her hand on my shoulder, and say, 'Those boys ain't your friends. I'm your friend. You remember that.'"

He smiled faintly. "She was kind of an entrepreneur, too. Her sweet potato pies were so good, neighbors used to argue on the porch about who deserved the last slice. I swear one time, Mr. Earl tried to trade his lawnmower just to get a pie fresh out of the oven. She'd sell them to try to make a little extra money, but she'd end up giving most of them away to people who needed a smile more than she needed the cash."

Bryce's voice was small but thoughtful. "Did she ever get tired, Dad? Taking care of everyone like that?"

Brian's eyes softened even more. "She never showed it. And even if she did, she'd just pray and keep going."

Brian's voice grew tender. "And she always told me, 'Treat others the way you want to be treated.' I've carried that with me my whole life."

Bryce leaned forward, completely lost in his father's words. "So... she made you believe?"

Brian nodded. "Every single day. Even when I didn't believe in myself, she did. She told me I was special, even when the world told me I wasn't worth a damn. And that's why I don't let you quit, Bryce. Because you come from a line of people who never gave up."

Bryce looked down at his hands, voice quiet. "I wish I could've met her."

Brian's eyes grew misty as a memory flashed across his mind. "One time, I came home bleeding after a fight I didn't start. I thought she'd be mad I got in trouble, but she cleaned me up in the kitchen, humming a hymn the whole time. Then she sat me down, made me a plate of fried chicken, and told me I was meant for bigger things than street corners. I never forgot that."

He took a slow breath, voice steady. "That's what I want you to understand, Bryce. One person's love can change everything. Grandma's belief in me made me try harder—even when life felt heavier than I thought I could handle. And that's what you gotta do, too. When things get tough, you try harder."

A beat of silence hung in the air until Leon leaned back, shaking his head. "Man, your grandma was tougher than half the dudes I know now. I'd have run from her faster than I ever ran from the cops."

Jackie snorted, wiping a tear with her thumb. "Ain't that the truth? I'd take a night in jail before a whooping from a grandma like that."

Trey pointed at Bryce with a grin. "Better listen close, kid. You think your dad's tough? Grandma would've had him sweeping the porch, peeling potatoes, and reciting Bible verses before breakfast."

The shop burst into low, warm laughter, breaking the heaviness like sunshine through clouds.

Bryce looked around, eyes wide but smiling. He hesitated, then asked softly, "But... even with Grandma... did you ever mess up?"

Brian's eyes darkened, memories shifting. He picked up the clippers, voice low and rough. "Let me tell you about the hood..."

Bryce couldn't wait to hear more. But he had no idea just how dangerous the next chapter would get.

hood.

The clippers buzzed low as Brian leaned in close, tightening a fresh taper on Bryce's side. Outside, sirens echoed faintly in the distance, a regular soundtrack. Inside the shop, Leon tossed a bottle of water from hand to hand, Jackie scrolled through her phone, and Trey tapped a beat on the armrest with his knuckles.

Bryce looked up at his dad through the mirror. "Dad... what was it like growing up where you did? Like, for real?"

Brian didn't answer right away. He clicked the clippers off and stared out the window. "You ever heard of the kind of place where everybody got dreams but nobody remembers them when they wake up?"

Leon smirked. "Sounds like DC in the 80s."

Jackie raised an eyebrow. "Baby, that was Chocolate City. And the only sweet part was the name."

Trey chuckled. "Before the cameras, before the apps, all you had was your rep, your word, and your eyes on the street."

Brian nodded slowly. "Exactly. And if you ain't had those, you were food."

Bryce leaned forward. "You were really around all that?"

Brian "Brian turned back to him. "Let me take y'all back..."

Back when I was little, we didn't have no internet. No YouTube. No phone to record what was wrong in your life. You had what you could see and what you could guess. And I didn't see much hope.

My mom was sick, but I didn't understand why at the time. I just knew she loved me and always tried her best. When I visited her, I didn't always like the neighborhood. We had lights. Food, although she couldn't cook like Grandma. A nice restaurant? A fancy dinner? That was a dream. But she was my mom, and I loved her. I didn't understand what "mental health" meant. I just knew some days she didn't get out of bed and other days she'd get up yelling at shadows that weren't there.

Grandma raised me. And at Grandma's house, there were always a lot of people in the house. Two, sometimes three folks sharing a full-sized bed. If you got tired of *smelling* feet all night..., you'd grab a blanket and post up on the floor. There was no such thing as leftovers — not because there wasn't enough food, but because family or friends would show up and eat it all right off the stove. You'd turn your head for five seconds, and your plate was gone. And your seat too. And don't even think about experiencing that meal again—Grandma only cooked certain dishes once a year.

We lived in a version of DC no postcard ever showed. You'd walk outside, and the first thing you heard was the sound of cop cars and ambulances. If it wasn't a fight, it was a raid. If it wasn't a raid, it was someone getting jumped over sneakers that weren't even in their size.

Kids didn't dream about college. They dreamed about getting a car with tinted windows, maybe a gold chain, and making enough money not to share their fries. We were all trying to figure out how to be somebody while surrounded by nobodies acting like they had it all figured out.

Go-go music pulsed from every corner. Backyard Band, Rare Essence, the real DC sound. It made you want to dance and throw hands at the same time. Sundays were for Redskins games, back when the name was still controversial, but nobody cared because we just wanted to win. Georgetown basketball was everything. We didn't even know where Georgetown was on a map, but we repped hard because that was our pride. Len Bias? Man, that was the dream and the heartbreak all in one, a legend taken too soon.

And don't get me started on Reaganomics. The president talking about trickle-down like it was a blessing. Only thing that ever trickled in my hood was tears and gunshots.

By the time we moved to PG County, things were supposed to feel different. People had more money. Nicer homes. But it was the same mentality. Everyone still stealing, lying, cheating. Wearing fake Jordans while judging someone else's outfit. Committing crimes for no reason. It was all a performance—just smoke and mirrors. Like we were all stuck in a lie, pretending this was progress.

They say it's the richest Black county in the country, but what does that even mean if the schools still trash, no grocery stores want to come, and everybody got to leave the county to get a decent meal or a clean mall? All the income in the world, but the mindset was still survival. That's what the hood teaches you. No matter how far you move, the trenches move with you if you don't fix what's inside.

Trey chimed in, shaking his head. "You just described my entire block growing up. We had Beamers parked on broken sidewalks.."

Jackie sipped her coffee. "And gold chains with overdue light bills."

Leon raised his hand like a toast. "Here's to the illusion of having it all."

Bryce blinked. "Wait... people still did crimes even when they had stuff?"

Brian smirked. "Son, where I come from, committing a crime wasn't about needing something. It was about not wanting to feel powerless. Even the kids with both parents and cable in every room were still out stealing bikes."

"You ever grow up in a place where everyone talks about making it out, but no one ever really leaves? That was the hood. A thousand dreams, but nobody knew the directions."

Bryce looked up. "So what made you different?"

Brian paused. "I didn't feel different. But something inside me—call it God, call it stubbornness, kept telling me: You don't belong here. Not in an arrogant way. More like... a whisper that wouldn't shut up. Something was telling me there was more of the world to see."

Bryce looked surprised. "Candy hustle?"

"We bought blow pops in bulk and moved them like mini moguls. Me and Vick thought we were CEOs, just with sticky fingers, cheap cologne, and a locker for an office."

Trey laughed. "You was slinging Jolly Ranchers, huh?"

"Until the vice principal hit a lick on our stash."

Leon wiped a tear. "They confiscated the candy?"

"Nah. They taxed it."

Jackie howled. "Straight extortion!"

Brian smiled. "I learned young — ain't no such thing as fair in the hood. Even the adults were playing dirty."

There were days I'd walk home past liquor stores, chicken joints, and carry-outs with bulletproof glass, just hoping I'd make it back before the streetlights came on. That was the code. The lights flicker? You better be inside. Or run like hell.

Bryce leaned in. "Were you scared?"

"Every day. But fear teaches you how to read people. Teaches you when to speak, when to stay silent, and when to disappear. You learn to carry yourself like you got something to lose, even when you don't."

Jackie sat back, quiet now.

Leon scratched his chin. "So how'd you not fall into it?"

Brian exhaled. "Honestly? I was too scared to get caught. And too stubborn to be average. And Grandma's disappointed face would break my heart."

Bryce, thoughtful: "So you just... made up your mind?"

"Eventually. But not before making a whole lotta dumb decisions."

Brian looked at his son in the mirror, hand still on the clippers. "Listen, Bryce. The hood don't just shape you. It tests what kind of shape you wanna be in. It don't care how smart you are. It don't care who your grandma was. It's gonna pull on you—until you either break... or push back."

Bryce took it in, silent.

Then Leon leaned back and said, "But y'all remember when Brian tried to sell fake Air Jordans behind the gym?"

Brian whipped around. "That was one time! And they weren't fake — they were... creative interpretations."

Jackie was doubled over laughing. "He called 'em 'Jumpman Juniors'!

Trey added, "Yo! I had a pair. The man was jumpin' over a shopping cart!"

The shop erupted in laughter. Even Bryce had tears in his eyes.

Brian grinned. "Alright, alright, y'all done clownin' me?"

Bryce, still smiling, looked up. "That's wild, Dad. I didn't know it was like that."

Brian nodded, the grin fading to something real. "That's why I tell these stories. Not so you feel bad. So you understand — what you come from, and what you don't have to go through."

He picked up the clippers again, the buzz filling the shop once more.

Bryce turned to him, soft: "What happened next?"

Brian smiled. "Let me tell you about church..."

Leon groaned. "Oh Lord, here we go..."

Jackie cackled. "Y'all ready for some holy trauma?"

Trey raised both hands. "I'll bring the tambourine."

They laughed as the clippers buzzed back on.

church.

Bryce had been unusually quiet all morning. He sat in the chair, fidgeting with his hoodie strings while Brian cleaned his clippers.

"You alright?" Brian asked, eyeing him in the mirror.

"Yeah. I mean..." Bryce shrugged. "You've told me a lot about Grandma and how you grew up. But you never really talk about church. Or God."

Brian looked up. "Boy, we didn't just *go* to church. We lived there. Might as well had a cot in the back with my name stitched on it."

Leon laughed from the corner. "Don't let him fool you, Bryce. Your dad was Church Famous. Had folks throwin' peppermints like confetti after his solos."

Jackie jumped in. "He was the original Kirk Franklin with a high-pitched Donnie McClurkin finish!"

Trey added, "Only kid I knew who could sing 'His Eye is on the Sparrow' and moonwalk out the pulpit."

Brian sighed, half laughing, half traumatized. "Y'all wild. But Bryce, since you asked... let me take you back."

Our church was called *Greater Mount Calvary Tabernacle of Joy and Deliverance (Third*

Bapticostal Edition). Nobody knew what all that meant. But it was the only building on the block with stained glass windows and a sign that flashed scripture like Vegas.

The pastor? Reverend Dr. Harold L. Witherspoon III. A man so dramatic, he once fainted mid-sermon from "spiritual exhaustion" — but caught himself on the pulpit and turned it into a praise break. He preached in parables and metaphors so thick, you needed a decoder ring from the usher board.

Grandma? She was the real minister. Her purse had mints, Kleenex, and judgment. She'd lean over mid-sermon and whisper scripture in my ear like threats.

"Spare the rod, spoil the child," she'd hiss if I so much as looked sleepy.

"Fools despise wisdom," she'd mutter loud enough for the whole row to hear if I wore my pants too low.

But she was love, too. She'd squeeze my hand during altar calls and whisper, "God has His hand on you, baby. Don't let the devil lease it out."

Now listen—one Sunday, I had a plan. I was gonna catch the Holy Ghost. I'd studied it. Practiced the footwork. Watched Sister Jenkins break into a full shout with her wig sliding like it was trying to escape. I was READY.

The organ hit, folks started clapping, and I stood up like it was my turn on Showtime at the Apollo.

Bryce leaned in, grinning. "What happened?"

Brian closed his eyes. "I sold out, man. Froze like a statue. The Spirit passed me like I wasn't even home. Deacon Wilson caught it behind me, ran straight into a plant."

Jackie cracked up. "You rehearsed the Holy Ghost?!"

Leon wiped tears. "That boy said not today, Spirit. Not today."

But the singing? Oh, I was that kid.

High-pitched, angelic. Like Michael Jackson with a Bible. People came from other churches just to hear me hit the final note on "His Eye is on the Sparrow." If TikTok existed back then, I'd be booked.

"These days, I'd be trending for sure. Probably have a TikTok challenge named after me: the BBT Holy Ghost Shuffle."

Then I hit puberty.

Bryce raised an eyebrow. "What happened?"

Brian sighed. "I opened my mouth and sounded like a car alarm and a dying cat in a duet. I lost the gift, just like that. The Lord giveth... and the Lord muteth."

Trey gasped, fake dramatic. "Tragic! A fallen falsetto!"

Brian shook his head. "I ain't been right since."

Still, Grandma made sure I understood church wasn't just a building. She said, "Faith ain't about performin'. It's about rememberin'. You remember who kept you, and you act like it."

Every Sunday, I would pray for my mom. I didn't even know how. Just closed my eyes real tight and asked God to make her better. Most days, she was. Some days, she wasn't. And after a while... I stopped asking. Not because I stopped believing—just because I didn't know if God was listening to kids like me.

And Bryce, I know you're science-minded. You like data and proof. But sometimes, all you got is belief. And when life gets hard—and it will—you gon' need somethin' bigger than facts to pull you through.

Bryce nodded slowly. "So... do you still believe?"

Brian smiled. "Every day. Not always in perfect ways. But in real ways."

Jackie folded her arms. "Well, now I want to hear you sing again."

Brian stood firm. "Ain't happening."

Leon pointed to the broom. "C'mon man, hit that high note. I'll be your mic stand."

Trey tapped the clippers like a tambourine. "'Eyeeeee is on the sparrowwwww!'"

Brian shook his head, laughing. "See, this is why people leave the church."

Bryce squinted. "Wait... so you peaked in church?"

The shop erupted.

Brian raised a hand. "Y'all want one more? Let me tell you about communion."

Jackie leaned in. "Oh this gon' be good."

Brian nodded. "One Sunday, somebody messed up. The communion juice wasn't grape juice. It was real wine. The teens in the back? Treatin' it like shots. Folks passed out, passed gas, passed judgment. That was the last time we had 'open table' communion."

Bryce was crying laughing. "Wait, they got drunk at church?"

"Lit for the Lord," Trey said, wiping tears.

Brian pointed at his son. "You would've loved Grandma, but she ain't play. You complain about waking up early to run—Grandma made me go to church eight days a week. Sunday service, Monday night prayer, Tuesday Bible study, Wednesday rehearsal, Thursday fast, Friday revival, and Saturday cleaning day. She wouldn't even let me sleep on her lap. You would've been miserable."

Bryce was still cracking up, but nodded.

Brian clicked the clippers back on.

"So... what came after all that?"

Brian grinned. "Girls."

Jackie groaned. "Oh Lawd, here we go."

Leon said, "Get the bleep button ready."

Trey crossed himself. "Bless this next chapter."

They all cracked up as Brian lined up the next memory.

girls.

Wale's "Pretty Girls" was blasting through the speakers. Bryce sat in the chair, flipping through his phone like he was solving an equation.

"Dad," he said, not looking up, "what's the deal with girls, man?"

Brian looked up from cleaning his clippers. "That's a broad question. You trying to date one, dodge one, or survive one?"

Trey chuckled. "Survive is the right word."

Leon leaned in. "Just one? Back in my day we were duckin' exes like dodgeballs."

Jackie rolled her eyes. "Y'all toxic."

Bryce shook his head. "It's just... it's wild out here. Social media, FaceTime, TikTok. You say one wrong thing, you on a group chat you ain't even in."

Brian laughed. "Man. I thought I had it bad. But you? You're growing up in a whole different war zone."

He clicked the clippers on, then off again.

"Let me take you back."

I was always cool. Just not loud, or a threat, or overly athletic. The game back then was for athletes, dope boys, or dudes with uncles who owned a barbershop. I wasn't in *any* of those categories.. I was quiet. Observant. Liked my own space. If I had headphones, a notebook, and a pair of clean sneakers, I was good.

I wasn't ugly — I just wasn't trying hard. Girls liked the dudes who got suspended, not the ones who got honor roll.

Even when I did get the girl I liked, I didn't know what to do with her. I'd spend weeks watching her from across the hallway, heart pounding like I was in a boxing match. Then finally work up the nerve to say something... and boom. She liked me back. Then I'd disappear. Ghosted before ghosting was a word.

Trey cackled. "You was out here rejecting blessings."

Brian nodded. "Because deep down, I didn't want attention. I wanted peace. But back then, peace wasn't popular."

Leon added, "Back then? Still ain't."

Jackie laughed. "Facts."

But that life... it wasn't built for kids like me. My grandma couldn't afford trainers or keep me in sports. So I wasn't athletic enough to stand out. And I damn sure wasn't going to commit a crime just to be seen. That meant I had to be fly in my own way.

And I was.

I'd rock the cleanest fit I could scrape together. Knew how to mix Payless with Marshall's like it was designer. My lineup was always sharp, shoes always clean. And even if I didn't talk much, when I did? You listened.

That's what got me by. Not swag. Strategy.

I was picky. Always have been. Even when I didn't know my worth, I knew my worth. Son—know your worth. Picking the wrong girl can lead to a lifetime of problems.

And the quiet dudes? They were getting all the girls. I never understood it. Now I do.

Although I was introverted, I was vocal. I always wanted the most popular girl—and *I* did get them. But I hated the obligation of walking her to class every day. It stole my freedom. And freedom? That's something I never gave up easy.

Bryce leaned forward. "So… you just didn't mess with girls like that?"

Brian shrugged. "I wasn't in the game. Didn't know the rules. But now? I understand women better than most."

Jackie raised an eyebrow. "Oh really?"

Brian nodded. "Because I paid attention. I listened. And I didn't fake who I was to impress anybody. That's the key."

He looked directly at Bryce.

"You smart. You athletic. Focus on that. Focus on you. Your sports. Your books. Your money. Build all that now. And when the girls start coming—and they will—do your due diligence. Learn and understand you first. That's how you find the right one."

He paused.

"Or… ones."

The shop howled.

Bryce laughed, shaking his head. "So what you saying is... play it smart?"

Brian smiled. "Exactly. Play it smart. And don't chase love in the ninth grade. Chase your greatness."

Jackie pointed her comb at Bryce. "And if you do get a girlfriend, tell her I want to meet her first."

Trey added, "Bring her to church. That's the real test."

Leon said, "Nah, let Grandma interview her from heaven. That woman had a sixth sense."

The shop laughed again as the clippers hummed.

Brian shook his head, smirking. "Man... let me tell you about Harvest Church."

Bryce raised an eyebrow. "Harvest what?"

"Harvest Church Summer Camp. Six weeks of confusion, fear, and delusion."

Jackie leaned in. "Ooh, this already sound like trauma."

"It was probably the most ghetto camp I've ever been to. They bussed in kids from every part of the hood hood. I swear, every day I feared for my life. The counselors? All ex-cons turned deacons. I ain't lying—one dude gave his testimony during snack time about how he used to hide razor blades in his gums."

Leon spit out his drink. "WHAT?"

Brian nodded. "I still flinch when I see Jello pudding."

"But even in chaos, your dad was on a mission. There was this girl—Lisa. A goddess. I knew by week six, she'd be mine. That's the thing with me and you, Bryce. We always want the top prize."

Bryce smiled. "Facts."

"The problem? I had no game, my shirt was two sizes too big, and my jeans had a thousand pockets and not one ounce of confidence. But I was determined. Every day, I built up the courage to say something. Little by little, she started talking back. We had chemistry. She even gave me a side hug once."

Jackie giggled. "Oh, it was serious-serious."

Brian continued, "She was always with her cousins—one of them definitely liked me. But I was focused. Zoned in. This was *my* camp love story. So on the final day, I walked Lisa and her cousins to the bus stop. This was it. My big moment. I was gonna go in for the kiss."

Trey clapped his hands. "Let's go!"

Brian held up a finger. "Except... right as I leaned in, Lisa turned to my boy—*my* boy—and kissed him like it was a rom-com finale. Right in front of me. I stood there like a groomsman with no speech. Then she got on the bus and left my life."

The whole shop erupted.

Leon shouted, "Oh no! Not the bus stop betrayal!"

Bryce was in tears. "Yo, you got curved on the finale!"

Brian nodded. "Lesson? Sometimes the top prize ain't yours. And the girl you ignoring? Probably the one bringing snacks to the group chat."

Jackie sipped her drink. "Friendship stories always got the most hurt."

Brian nodded. "That's 'cause the ones closest to you know exactly where to cut."

friends.

Bryce was still cracking up from the summer camp story. "Yo, you really got curved like that?"
Brian nodded. "Final episode. No credits. Just heartbreak."
Leon wiped a tear. "Camp love gone wrong, man."
Jackie raised an eyebrow. "That girl ever come back?"
Brian shook his head. "Never saw her again."
Bryce smirked. "Dang... first the girl curved you, now your boys?"
Brian paused. "Whew. That's a whole other type of pain."

He clicked the clippers off and looked into the mirror. "Let's talk about friendship."

See, with girls? You kinda expect drama. But your friends? That's supposed to be your people. Your safe zone. Your co-defendants in life. But that ain't always how it went.

The problem wasn't that I didn't have friends. The problem was... everybody was fake. Smiling in your face, but plotting behind your back. Acting real, but moving funny. That's why loyalty always meant more to me than popularity.

"I had this boy once. His name was Devin. We grew up next door to each other and did everything together. Bike rides, hoops, even random arguments over who was faster or who got next on the game. We fought almost every day. But it was never real. He'd punch me in the arm. I'd say I was gonna get him back. Then we'd be laughing again in five minutes."

Jackie raised an eyebrow. "So y'all were best friends?"

"I thought so. Even when he started dating this girl I liked, I stayed loyal. He didn't do nothing wrong... he didn't know. But still, it stung. I let it go."

Leon added, "Bet you ain't let it go internally though."

Brian smirked. "Not at all."

He clicked the clippers off.

His family was the opposite of mine. At my house, somebody was always yelling, fighting, or stepping over cousins sleeping on the floor. But at his house? Quiet. Structured. Just him, his mom, his dad, and a sister. They were from the Islands. His pops was an engineer—or something like that. Smart, serious dude. Every time I came over, he'd give me a nod and say, "Turner."

I'd say, "Hi?"

And he'd go, "What do you mean 'hi'?" and walk off.

Every time. For years.

I used to ask my boy what I was supposed to say. He'd shrug and go, "I don't know." I never figured it out.

The shop broke into laughter.

Leon said, "That man was operating on a different frequency."
Brian nodded. "Still don't know if I passed or failed a test."
Jackie wiped a tear. "What happened to Devin?"
Brian's face turned soft. "He moved. And we lost touch."
Bryce frowned. "Man. So basically, you was just getting curved left and right—by girls and boys."
The whole shop hollered.
Trey pointed. "Put that on a t-shirt: Curved by Everybody."

Grandma used to say, "Your family is your best friend." I didn't fully get it at the time. But now I do.

She used to say it while folding laundry, not even looking up—like it was just a fact of life, not a lesson.

Years later, he popped back up. Reached out. We hung for a little, just wasn't the same.

The biggest lesson I learned was out of sight, out of mind.
I wasn't mad anymore. Once I understood the truth, I moved on.

Bryce nodded again, this time slower—like something clicked.

Brian looked at him. "You'll see what I mean. It starts small. A friend copies your homework. Borrows your hoodie and never returns it. Cracks a joke about you in front of a girl. And next thing you know, they not who you thought."

Brian smiled, shook his head, then leaned forward again—like the memory had just tapped him on the shoulder.

"Let me tell y'all another one. When I was little, the spot was 7-Eleven. Not for Slurpees—for video games. Super Mario Bros. I was a beast. I'd be in there for hours and folks would gather around just to watch. I had groupies before puberty."

The shop laughed.

Brian continued, "So one summer, I finally got a new bike. Not a Mongoose or a Huffy—we didn't have it like that. Mine was white, beautiful, and came from Zayre. Or one of those stores. I loved that bike. So every time I went to 7-Eleven, I'd lock it up and run inside. Thought I was good. All the kids outside? That was my crew."

Jackie smirked. "Oh no. I feel a betrayal coming."

Brian nodded. "One day, after a grueling Mario session, I walked outside and boom—front tire gone. Just gone! They ain't take the whole bike. Just the tire. That hurt worse. Bike looked like a wounded animal."

Leon hollered. "Not the one-wheeler!"

Trey added, "Them ain't your boys, man. That's a lesson!"

Brian grinned. "That's when I learned—everybody cheering you on ain't cheering for you. Some just waiting to catch you slippin'."

Bryce let out a slow "Daaaamn…"

Brian looked at him. "That's why I always say—pay attention to energy, not words. And don't confuse time with trust."

Jackie stirred her drink. "Friendship stories always got the most hurt."

Brian nodded. "Told y'all last time—it's always the ones closest to you that know where to cut."

sports.

Some Bobby Womack was playing low in the background—one of those old soulful joints that made the whole room feel like Sunday morning.

Bryce sat back in the chair, fresh out of practice, towel around his neck. He pulled at his shoelaces, still catching his breath from the heat outside.

"Dad..." he said between exhales, "you were into sports, right? Were you good?"

Brian looked up from cleaning his clippers. "Depends who you ask."

The shop chuckled.

Leon leaned forward. "Oh Lord, not this again."

Jackie raised an eyebrow. "We talkin' track, football, basketball—what?"

Bryce grinned. "All of it. I'm just tryna picture you back then. Like... were you *nice*?"

Brian smirked. "I played."

He clicked the clippers on for a quick buzz, then flicked them back off.

"But I was never seen."

Trey pointed his comb like a mic. "Bet you had game, OG! Droppin' 30 a night!"

Brian grinned wide. "Game? I *swear* I had the nastiest crossover... in my head. I ran the ball like Eric Dickerson. High knees! I remember running 80 yards in the rain, jumping over a defender, and takin' it to the house. Man, I was a bad boy."

Leon laughed. "In your mind, you was Barry Sanders and Jordan rolled into one!"

Jackie shook her head. "Sounds like you averaged 50 fantasy points a game!"

Brian cracked up. "Star? I tried cross country once. First day, they made us run a few miles. Halfway through, I threw up and quit the next day."

He looked at Bryce, half-serious. "See, son? Don't be a loser like your dad."

The shop *exploded* in laughter. Leon slapped the armrest, Jackie wiped tears from her eyes.

Trey said through his laugh, "Man, you had every sport covered — in your dreams!"

Brian leaned back. "Hey, my dreams were undefeated!"

Jackie pointed at him. "And reality was handing you L's."

More laughter filled the shop—loud, but warm. The kind that lived between the lines of truth and love.

Brian leaned forward, his voice a bit lower now. "Let me tell y'all somethin'. Ninth grade? I made the JV basketball team... but I didn't play a single game."

Jackie blinked. "Wait—why not?"

"Because I didn't even check the list," Brian said. "Didn't think I made it. I walked right past the paper on the wall—twice. Couldn't bring myself to look. I just assumed I got cut and never showed up."

Leon leaned in. "Wait... so you was on the team and didn't even know?"

Brian nodded slowly. "Yeah. People told me later. But by then, it was too late. I missed my shot."

The shop went quiet for a second.

"Back then, I'd never played real organized ball. We ain't have money for leagues or trainers. My friends had travel teams and uniforms. Me? I had cracked sidewalks and a busted Spalding."

No trainers. No gear. No blueprint. Just drive.

Trey nodded. "So what happened after that?"

Brian continued, "Tenth grade came around, and I wasn't about to make the same mistake twice. I showed up. Didn't know nobody. Coach ain't know my name. I was just some skinny kid from nowhere."

He smiled faintly. "But I made it. Again. And this time, I stayed. Started out at the bottom in preseason—last option. But by the start of the season? I was the starting point guard."

For the first time in my life playing organized ball, I wasn't invisible. I had a jersey. A role. A name on the board.

Bryce raised his eyebrows. "For real?"

Brian nodded. "Played the whole year. Earned everything."

Jackie asked, "And the coaching?"

Brian laughed once, bitter. "Rough. No room for mistakes. You mess up, you're benched and embarrassed. Coaches were like drill sergeants. Cold. I didn't learn plays—I learned how to survive."

Leon said, "That's the stuff they don't show in highlight reels."

Brian nodded. "Facts. And I trained on my own. Sunrise to sundown. Pushups in my room. Dribbled in the driveway, and shot the ball up against the middle brick until Grandma yelled to bring my ass in the house."

Bryce nodded again, this time slower—like something finally clicked.

Brian looked away for a beat, his voice lower now. "When the dream died..."

He paused, eyes darker now.
"And I almost answered."

The shop was silent.

"I still remember scanning that varsity list—twice—and never seeing my name. I missed school for a week."

He let the silence sit.

"I remember being stuck in my room, listening to Walter Hawkins, trying to lift my spirits. Nothing worked. I wasn't hungry. ...Just laid there thinking...

it was over. No scholarships. No college. Just the same block, same struggle."

He glanced at Bryce, but his eyes drifted away again—back to that moment.

"My uncle—he was a pastor—came in one day, sat at the edge of my bed, and said, 'Winners never quit. Quitters never win.' I know that sounds cliché now... but back then? I had never heard that before. And it hit me hard."

Jackie said softly, "That'll shake you up."

Brian nodded. "Because it wasn't just about basketball. I thought that was my only shot to get out the hood. I believed the lie. That if I didn't make it on the court, I had no other way out."

He paused, letting that truth settle.

"But low and behold... it was a blessing in disguise. My focus changed. My mind expanded. I started seeing past the game—started seeing *me*. From that moment forward, I think I got all A's. I locked in."

Leon shook his head. "Man..."

Brian looked over at Bryce. "That's the trap. They make you believe your body is your only asset. That you gotta jump high, run fast, hit hard—to be somebody. And when it crumbles? You blame yourself. Not the system. Not the odds. *You*."

Trey added, "Especially for us. Ball ain't just a sport—it's an escape plan."

Brian nodded. "Exactly. But the numbers don't lie. Less than 2% of high school athletes get a D1 scholarship. Less than 1% go pro. And who's really filling up those rosters? Not kids like me. Not the ones without trainers. Or money. Or connections."

Bryce stayed quiet, but something in his expression shifted.

Brian continued, voice steady now. "When that dream died, the streets came knocking."

He leaned back in his chair, eyes distant.

"And I almost answered."

Brian took a breath, then smiled faintly.

"But that's why I'm different now with y'all. I see how this stuff creeps in early."

He looked over at Bryce, then nodded toward the photo wall by the register—where a picture of Bria aka Bri Bri, the other BBT, in her volleyball jersey hung slightly crooked.

"Bri Bri just started volleyball."

Leon smiled. "The assassin in braids?"

Brian laughed. "Yep. First practice, she missed every serve. Second one? Same thing. She came home, slammed the door, and said, 'I'm trash. I quit.'"

Jackie chuckled. "Ain't that the way."

"I walked in and found her staring at her shoes like they betrayed her. You know what I told her?"

"What?" Trey asked.

"'You're not supposed to be great yet. You're supposed to be new. You learn. You show up. That's the win.'"

She asked me after practice... 'Did you ever feel like quitting too?' I just smiled. 'Every day. But I didn't. And neither will you.'

Bryce nodded slowly.

Brian turned to him. "That's what they don't tell you. Sports teach you how to show up for yourself—even when it hurts. Even when nobody's watching."

Jackie said, "So what'd she do?"

Brian smiled. "She went back the next day. Got one serve in. Just one. And I cheered like she won a championship."

Brian leaned back in the chair, eyes still distant. The room was quiet, each man holding something behind their silence.

Then, slowly, Bryce sat up.

He didn't say much. Just nodded again—this time slower, like something finally clicked.

He looked at the clippers in Brian's hand. Then at the shop. Then at his dad.

"Sports won't save me," he said quietly, "but they can shape me… right?"

Brian met his son's eyes. No jokes this time. Just pride.

"Exactly."

Leon exhaled. "Sheesh. I felt that one."

Trey: "Lil' man soundin' like he got a 4.0 and a fade!"

Jackie wiped an invisible tear. "That's growth right there."

Brian watched Bryce for a second longer. "Quiet kid. But he's listening. He's really listening."

Brian smiled to himself as he clicked the clippers back on.

"Now hold still before I mess up this lineup."

The hum of the clippers returned, low and steady.

Some Bobby Womack still played in the background.

And for a moment—just a moment—everything felt aligned.

crime.

It started like any other Saturday—clippers buzzing, music low, and the shop full of stories nobody's mama was supposed to hear.

Jackie shook his head, laughing. "Man, I remember the first time I got caught stealing. I was like eight. Thought I was slick—tucked some Now and Laters in my sock. Clerk saw the whole thing."

Leon grinned. "In the sock? Rookie move."

Trey leaned over. "Y'all ever steal somethin' and then try to return it 'cause you felt guilty?"

Everyone turned.

"Nope," they all said in unison.

The shop erupted.

Bryce raised an eyebrow. "Wait... y'all really used to steal?"

Brian didn't laugh. He just leaned back in his chair, eyes scanning the ceiling like a projector was flickering up there.

"Oh, I stole," he said calmly. "Candy. Toys. A CD or two from Sam Goody."

"Sam Goody?!" Jackie jumped in.

"But I'll say this..." Brian continued, "The only reason I didn't end up in real trouble was Grandma. Her voice stayed in my head like a soundtrack. She used to say..."

He paused, looking at Bryce.

"If you gotta hide it, you already know you wrong."

The room quieted for a beat.

"I remember being in 7-Eleven, probably around Bryce's age. I'd just figured out how to slide a Laffy Taffy up my sleeve without making noise. Heart pounding like I was robbing a bank, palms sweaty, pretending I was lookin' at gum."

Leon laughed. "You had a whole candy heist planned out!"

"Man, I'd walk up to the counter like I was just buying a single Blow Pop. Meanwhile I had like three packs of Now and Laters tucked in my hoodie."

Jackie raised an eyebrow. "And they ain't catch you?"

"Oh, they did. A few times. One clerk chased me out the store—I ducked behind a trash can like I was in Mission Impossible."

Bryce chuckled. "So you was out here runnin' drills."

Brian grinned. "Look, I wasn't built for crime. I got anxiety. But the real reason I never crossed the line? Grandma."

He leaned forward.

"Even when I was out there actin' wild, her voice stayed with me. That's what saved me. I stole some candy, yeah. Might've skipped school once or twice. But I could never hurt nobody."

He pointed to his chest.

"'Cause I still had a heart. And her voice lived in it."

Brian leaned back in the chair, eyes distant now.

"But that was kid stuff. The deeper it got, the more real it got."

He rubbed his hands together slowly, like the memory still lived in his palms.

"I still remember this one day in Kaywood Gardens. Summer. Humid. We was all out there—me, Joey, Billy—playin' throwback football. No pads, just bruises. I jumped over this one dude for a touchdown and hit the Cabbage Patch like I just scored in the Super Bowl. Next play, I got tackled so hard I thought my ribs cracked. I swear they still sore to this day."

Leon laughed. "Man, y'all used to play like y'all had insurance."

Brian smirked. "That was the code—no crying, no running home. Slap boxing settled everything. Get popped, shake it off, dap it up. That was normal. We learned how to take a hit—physically, emotionally—before we ever learned algebra."

The room nodded. Even Bryce.

"But that day? It turned wild. In the middle of the game, we heard screeching tires. Two cars flying up the narrow street—one red, one yellow. Kids started cheering like it was a parade."

Jackie's eyes widened. "Hold up. Was that—"

"Yup," Brian said. "Joey and Billy. Stole two damn Corvettes. Just... joyriding like it was Mario Kart. Cops were on 'em heavy, but those fools knew the neighborhood better than GPS. Cut through an alley, ditched the cars, and came sprinting past us like nothin' happened."

He shook his head slowly, voice lower now.

"That was the first time I saw how close it could get. Just one choice away. A little more speed. A wrong turn. A cop with a short fuse. And their lives woulda been done."

He looked at Bryce.

Bryce said, "What??"

"And I was right there. I wasn't in the car, but I was right there."

The shop fell quiet.

Brian took a breath.

"None of us thought it was crazy at the time. It was just... Tuesday."

The room went silent.

"See, I did dumb stuff—stole, lied, skipped school. But deep down? I couldn't cross that line. I couldn't hurt nobody. Couldn't stomach real crime. That was Grandma again."

He smiled faintly.

"She didn't even have to beat me. Just her voice... that was enough. Saved me more than once."

Brian leaned forward again, elbows on his knees.

"I ain't gon' lie. A lot of dudes I grew up with? They ain't make it. Some locked up. Some buried. Some still out there, tryna out-hustle time."

He looked over at Bryce.

"I had close calls. Situations that could've gone left real fast. But I never crossed that line. You know why?"

Bryce shook his head.

Brian pointed upward.
"Grandma. Her voice. Her prayers. Her disappointment."
He paused.
"I couldn't face her if I ever did something real foul. That's what kept me from becoming someone I couldn't come back from."

He exhaled. Slowly.

And somewhere in the stillness, faint but clear—
Grandma's voice echoed:
"God don't bless no mess."

That line hung in the air like smoke.
The shop got quiet again—this time, out of respect.

Then Bryce spoke, voice soft but clear.

"So doing wrong is easy... but staying right takes work?"

Brian smiled, proud. "Exactly."

The clippers buzzed back to life.

The sound filled the shop like a reset button.

Jackie glanced over, nodding. "Lil' man getting wise."

Leon added, "Whole shop about to end up with degrees at this rate."

Trey laughed. "A 4.0 and a rap sheet of wisdom."

Brian grinned, but didn't say much.

Just kept cutting.

And somewhere in the background, Grandma's voice lingered—quiet, but never gone.

college.

Some days, the shop was louder than the clippers. But today?

Today was different.

Brian stood at his station, cleaning his tools slower than usual, like something was on his mind.

Bryce sat in the chair, scrolling through his phone. He looked up casually.

"Dad... do I have to go to college?"

Brian froze mid-swipe.

Jackie looked up. "Ooh... that's a big one."

Leon muttered, "Better answer that right."

Brian stared at Bryce for a second. The question landed harder than it sounded.

He exhaled. "You don't even realize you just unlocked a whole chapter of trauma."

Trey smirked. "So what'd you say?"

Brian shook his head. "Didn't yet. But that question? Took me back."

Brian exhaled slowly through his nose. "There was a time I thought college wasn't even in the cards."

Leon raised an eyebrow. "That real?"

Brian nodded. "Man... Lincoln Tech had a recruiter in my living room. Sat right on the couch like he paid rent. Bro had a folder, a slideshow, and a fake smile like he was sellin' vacuums door-to-door."

Trey laughed. "You almost went?"

"I was close. The man had me convinced I'd be fixin' engines and air conditioners by Christmas. Said I'd be "in demand in every major city in America." Made it sound like I was about to join the Avengers."

Jackie leaned in. "What stopped you?"

Brian shrugged. "I think... deep down, I wanted more. But I won't lie—sometimes I wonder if that would've been smarter. Less debt. Less stress. I'd probably own a mechanic shop by now."

Leon smirked. "Yeah, but would you still be in the barbershop preachin' to the youth?"

Brian grinned. "Fair."

Then his smile faded a little.

"Truth is, college wasn't about dreams — it was about escape. I didn't care what school, what major. I just needed out. Out the house. Out the hood. Out the cycle."

He paused.

"But we ain't have money like that. FAFSA felt like a lottery ticket. And every brochure looked like it came with a $60,000 bill."

Brian leaned back in the chair, smirking. "Y'all ever try to skip class and still end up learning somethin'?"

Leon chuckled. "Ain't that the goal?"

Brian shook his head. "Nah. I mean... like God got jokes."

The shop leaned in.

"It was senior year. I had my whole plan mapped out — skip music class, hit the corner store, grab a slice and a soda, and chill by the field till third period. Easy."

Trey laughed. "Straight delinquent behavior."

"I was a pro," Brian said. "Until the day it all fell apart. I'm out there, mid-bite, greasy napkin in one hand, orange soda in the other... when I hear a voice behind me."

He paused for effect.

"'Brian Turner!' Like thunder cracking behind me."

Jackie gasped. "Not the full name!"

"Oh yeah. I turned around slow... and there she was. Ms. Riggins. My music teacher. Church lady. Always wore those orthopedic shoes and had a purse big enough to carry judgment, a hymnal, and half a Sunday dinner."

Leon said, "You was caught!"

"Caught?" Brian laughed. "She marched me back through the halls like a prisoner of war. Pizza in hand. Everybody watching. She didn't even say a word till we got back to the classroom."

Trey wiped his eyes. "Oh, this is gettin' good."

Brian nodded. "She sat me down. Looked me dead in the face. And said, 'I know you think this school doesn't matter. But you got more in you than you let people see. Don't be the reason your story stops here.'"

The shop went quiet.

"She pulled out this yellow folder. Told me about a grant. Said it wasn't much—but it was enough to get me through the door."

Jackie leaned in. "Wait—so the same teacher who caught you skippin'..."

"Yep," Brian said. "The same woman who caught me skippin' is the reason I went to college." If she hadn't stopped me that day, I probably wouldn't have even applied. Sometimes the detour *is* the blessing."

Leon shook his head. "That's wild."

He gave a short laugh. "Real wild."

Brian leaned back in his chair, voice softer now—almost like he was talking to himself.

"That grant Ms. Riggins told me about?" He shook his head, almost in disbelief. "Full ride. Covered everything. That woman changed my life with one sentence and a slice of pizza."

Leon blinked. "Wait, you got a full ride?"

Brian said, "It started as a full ride. I fumbled later... but that's a story for another book."

"Yeah. Whole thing. Tuition, books, housing—all of it. I didn't even know what 'financial aid' really meant until that moment. Nobody had broken it down for me before."

Jackie whistled. "Man..."

"But here's the crazy part," Brian continued, "I actually had the chance to go to a better school. More money, bigger campus, all that. But I turned it down."

Bryce looked up. "Why?"

Brian hesitated.

"Because I was scared. Thought I wasn't ready. Thought I didn't belong. I didn't know anybody who went away to school. I was one of the first in my family even talking about college. So I picked the safe one. Close to home. Familiar."

He stared at the floor for a moment.

"Sometimes I wonder if I sold myself short. But maybe... maybe I just did what I needed to do to survive."

Bryce nodded slowly.

"So you weren't even trying to go to college?" he asked.

Brian chuckled. "Nah. Not at all. I didn't think it was for people like me."

A pause.

"Even my school was underfunded and overcrowded, with textbooks held together by tape and prayers." But it still helped. There were people in there—like that music teacher—who saw me. And sometimes, one person seeing you is all it takes."

The room fell quiet again.

Then, softly, Grandma's voice floated through Brian's memory—equal parts holy and hilarious:

"You think you slick, but God got eyes everywhere."

Jackie cracked up. "Ain't that the truth."

Leon chuckled. "Even at the pizza spot."

Brian smiled. "Especially at the pizza spot."

The laughter faded gently, replaced by a silence that wasn't heavy—just real.

Bryce adjusted in the chair.

"So college wasn't the dream," he said. "But it became the step."

Brian nodded. "Exactly."

Then he clicked the clippers back on.

The buzz filled the shop again, warm and steady.

Bobby Womack hummed low in the background.

And just like that...
they were back in the cut.

reflections.

Ten cuts. Ten convos. One chair.
And somehow, my son ain't just walkin' out with a fresh fade, he's walkin' out with something more.

I didn't plan any of this—I wasn't trying to preach. But somewhere between the buzz of the clippers and the beat of the stories... truth showed up. And I realized, I'm not just teaching Bryce, I'm remembering me.

That's what this book is.
Not a memoir. Not a manual.
Just one dad tryna pass down what no one passed to him. One story at a time.

Because in our community, barbershops have been classrooms. And if we don't sit down and talk to our kids, really talk, the world will do it for us. Loud, reckless, and unfiltered. I'd rather he hear it from me.

And if you're reading this, maybe you're Bryce.
Maybe you're me.
Either way, just know:
You don't have to be perfect to be present.
You don't need answers to share your truth.
Sometimes, showing up *is* the lesson.

So that's ten stories.
But Bryce ain't done askin'.

He leaned forward the other day, eyes serious, voice
low—
"Okay, Dad... but did you stay?"

Book Two's gonna answer that.

But first?

Let the clippers cool off.

about.

Brian B. Turner is a writer, entrepreneur, and father who built his life from scratch—no handouts, no roadmap, just faith, hustle, and vision. Raised between Washington, D.C. and Prince George's County, Maryland, Brian's journey has taken him from cracked sidewalks and crowded apartments to boardrooms, barbershops, and business ownership.

He's the founder of several ventures, including Right at Home (a home care company) and hey BBT, a personal brand rooted in storytelling, resilience, and betting on yourself. But more than anything, Brian is a believer in the power of honest conversations—especially between fathers and sons.

BBT's Barbershop is his debut work in a series that blends humor, life lessons, and raw truth—capturing the voices of the past while shaping the minds of the future. He wrote it for his son Bryce, his daughter Bria, and every kid who's trying to find their way in a world that doesn't always make it easy.

When he's not writing or building, Brian's probably cracking jokes, closing deals, or cutting through the noise with another story worth telling.

acknowledgments.

To God—for the vision, the voice, and the grace to keep going when I wanted to give up.

To my children, Bryce and Bria—your love, your laughs, your questions, your dreams... you're the reason I fight. This book started as a conversation with you. Thank you for making me a better man, even when I fall short.

To Grandma Marie Simmons—your voice still guides me. Your prayers still cover me. Everything I am is built on your strength.

To my family, both by blood and by bond—thank you for the stories, the scars, and the survival. Each chapter holds a piece of you.

To my creative team—you know who you are. From late-night edits to early brainstorms, thank you for believing in this project and pushing me to the finish line.

To the barbershops that raised me—in D.C., in PG County, in every corner where Black men gather and grow—this one's for you.

And finally, to the kid out there who thinks they ain't seen, heard, or meant for more: You are. Keep going. Bet on yourself.

With love and gratitude,
Brian B. Turner